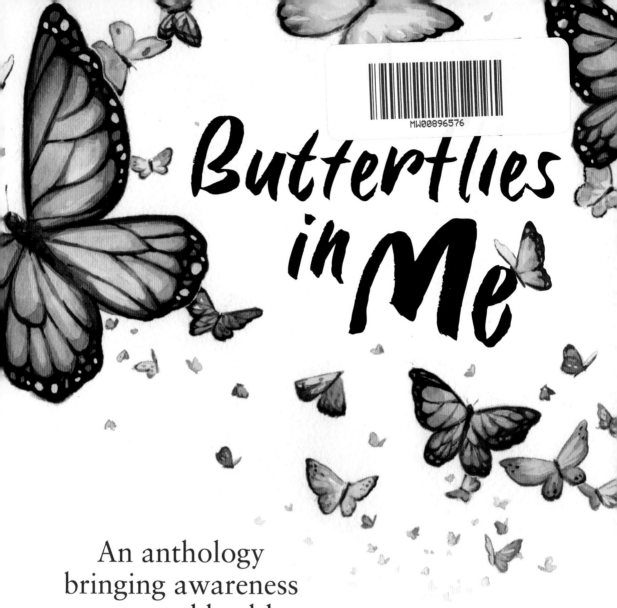

Butterflies in Me

An anthology
bringing awareness
to mental health

BOYS TOWN
Press®

Boys Town, Nebraska

Written by **Denisha Seals**
Illustrated by **Gabhor Utomo**

Butterflies in Me
Text and Illustrations Copyright © 2022 by Father Flanagan's Boys' Home
ISBN: 978-1-944882-83-9

Published by the Boys Town Press
13603 Flanagan Blvd.
Boys Town, NE 68010

For a Boys Town Press catalog, call **1-800-282-6657**
or visit our website: **BoysTownPress.org**

Publisher's Cataloging-in-Publication Data

Names: Seals, Denisha, author. | Utomo, Gabhor, illustrator.

Title: Butterflies in me : an anthology bringing awareness to mental health / written by Denisha Seals ; illustrated by Gabhor Utomo.

Other titles: Learning to love you butterfly: a workbook building self-esteem and resilience and Tools for children to embrace their mental health: companion material to supplement Butterflies in Me anthology

Identifiers: ISBN: 978-1944882-83-9 (text) | 978-1-944882-84-6 (workbook) | 978-1-944882-85-3 (companion supplement)

Subjects: LCSH: Abused children--Mental health--Juvenile fiction. | Abused teenagers--Mental health--Juvenile fiction. | Child mental health--Juvenile fiction. | Teenagers--Mental health--Juvenile fiction. | Self-esteem in children--Juvenile fiction. | Self-esteem in adolescence--Juvenile fiction. | Resilience (Personality trait) in children--Juvenile fiction. | Resilience (Personality trait) in adolescence--Juvenile fiction. | Social acceptance in children--Juvenile fiction. | Vulnerability (Personality trait)--Juvenile fiction. | Emotions in children--Juvenile fiction. | Emotions in adolescence--Juvenile fiction. | Depression in children--Juvenile fiction. | Depression in adolescence--Juvenile fiction. | Abused children--Mental health--Handbooks, manuals, etc. | Abused teenagers--Mental health--Handbooks, manuals, etc. | Self-care, Health--Handbooks, manuals, etc. | CYAC: Abused children--Fiction. | Abused teenagers-- Fiction. | Mental health--Fiction. | Self-esteem--Fiction. | Resilience (Personality trait)-- Fiction. | Social acceptance--Fiction. | Emotions--Fiction. | Depression--Fiction. | Self-care, Health. | BISAC: JUVENILE FICTION / Social Themes / Physical & Emotional Abuse. | JUVENILE FICTION / Social Themes / Depression & Mental Illness. | JUVENILE FICTION / Diversity & Multicultural.

Classification: LCC: PZ7.1.S336886 B88 2022 | DDC: [FIC]--dc23

Printed in the United States
10 9 8 7 6 5 4 3 2 1

Boys Town Press is the publishing division of Boys Town, a national organization serving children and families.

Dear Reader,

A butterfly is strong enough to brush against
the strongest winds but also beautifully fragile if you
tug on its wings. When I think of a child with mental
illness, I think of that child as a butterfly, strong yet fragile.
The butterfly – unique, vibrant, and animated with color –
represents children overcoming mental illness. When I was a child,
I suffered from PTSD. As an adult, I still cope with its effects on my
mind, body, and spirit. As an author, I want to create a discussion
among multiple communities that often do not understand mental
health due to misconceptions and stigmas.

I am grateful and hopeful that this book will give you some insight
on how you are special and strong, and you did nothing wrong.

You're truly a butterfly, spread your wings and take on the world.
Fly, butterfly, fly!

– DENISHA SEALS

WHAT'S BEING SAID ABOUT BUTTERFLIES IN ME:

Butterflies in Me includes short, fictional vignettes about
multicultural children experiencing various forms of
distress, including depression, grief, ADHD, and PTSD. In each
story, the child is appropriately confused and worried about his or
her symptoms. The vignettes conclude with the children receiving help
from culturally-appropriate sources, including faith healers, doctors,
and counselors. In each case, the children learn that their difficulties
are common, can be helped, and that their distress is not their fault.
This is an important message to communicate to those experiencing
any form of emotional distress. Minorities are disproportionately
impacted by mental health problems, disproportionately underserved
by mental health resources, and experience high rates of stigma. Not
only does this book attempt to normalize distress among minority
populations, but it demonstrates how even the most fragile among us
can get effective services if needed.

– ADAM C. MILLS, PH.D.
  Psychology Department, Nebraska Medicine

My name is Javier Sanchez.

I'm 14 years old. I'm the captain of my school's soccer team. So many people call me their friend. I receive awards for getting good grades.

I love being at school. It's my safe place. I have a secret admirer, but I am too shy to ask her on a date.

When I have to leave my favorite place, I'm always sad.

I'll tell you a secret. I'm tired of my mom and me getting beaten up by my stepdad.

Javier Sanchez

I beg Mom to pack up so we can leave. She says, "Mijo, we cannot. We have no place to go to be free."

We had nowhere to go. My mother is an only child, and my grandparents passed away a long time ago. My stepdad moved us away from all of my mom's friends. Mom would always cover her bruises with makeup. She always apologized to him, even if she did nothing to upset him. I think she tried to keep the peace in the house to avoid the fights, so she just did what he said. He made Mom wear her hair in an updo style. She was even forced to look down at the floor when he spoke to her. I even heard him say, "That's what guilty dogs do when they displease their masters."

He made us feel like the dirt on the ground people walk all over. I hated the way he treated her, the way he spoke to her and, most of all, I hated having to pretend we were the perfect family. I would stand up for Mom, but she told me to stop because that made his anger worse!

I covered up my blue and black bruises and hoped they would blend into my soccer uniform. A teacher asked me why my grades were falling. I told her a lie. I said, "Mrs. Carroll, everything is fine."

Everything was not fine. Days, weeks, and months went by, and everything still was not fine. One day, Mrs. Carroll told me to stay behind while the other kids went to lunch.

She told me she knew my black eye was not from playing too rough on the soccer field. She told me I was safe and could tell her what was wrong. She even said she could make the problem go away. But I was afraid.

I told her the black eye was not from rough play. It was from my stepdad, and I was afraid. She took me to the school nurse and asked me if the principal could join us. She told me not to be afraid because I did nothing wrong.

I showed them my scars and bruises. I told them stories of what made him angry enough to do bad things to me. They called the police who then went to my house to ask Mom if the stories I told were true. Mom was also afraid. She said if they promised to take us to a safe place, she would tell them the truth.

They took my stepdad away, and Mom held me and said we're finally free. When the police took us to the hospital to make sure our wounds would heal, Mom and I held each other's hands tightly. During the doctor's physical exams, Mom could tell I was afraid. She smiled at me, but I knew she was scared too.

After our exams, the hospital's social worker spoke to us. Her name was Mrs. Juanita Hernandez. She said it was her job to make sure we were safe. Mrs. Hernandez said we needed to live at a shelter for domestic violence victims. She promised us that the shelter's location was secret, and there were safety guidelines and rules that even we had to follow for our protection and the protection of others at the shelter.

At the shelter, Mom would go through something called a self-sufficiency program that would allow us to be independent. After completing the program, we would have housing, transportation, and opportunities for Mom to further her education.

My mother agreed and after six months of living in the shelter, we were finally approved for housing. It was nice to finally be in my own room, cook in my own kitchen, and play soccer in my own yard. Days, weeks, and months went by, but everything still was not fine. I had nightmares about my stepdad coming back to hurt me and Mom, though he never did. I didn't understand the nightmares because I was safe in my new home with my mom. I knew he could never find us!

I had flashbacks of what he did. I would cry, cry, and cry all the time. Mom reached out to Mrs. Juanita, and she suggested I go to a child therapist. The therapist's name was Mr. Julio Puente, and he diagnosed me with Post Traumatic Stress Disorder, or PTSD. I didn't know what that meant. He explained that the brain never forgets good or bad things, and sometimes the brain can become confused about what is happening in the present because of pain from the past.

Mr. Puente and Mom told me that I was special, strong, and I did nothing wrong.

Mom said she will be beside me every step of the way, so I no longer have to be afraid. Mr. Puente told me that weekly therapy sessions with him will help my brain heal so I can live a healthy and happy life. He said he would be able to give me the tools to help me throughout my healing process. He gave me books to read about my condition to help me understand better. He introduced me to children who went through similar experiences so we could lean on each other and possibly create friendships.

I remind myself, "I am special, strong, and I did nothing wrong. ***Fly, butterfly, fly!***"

My name is Kenya Olew.
I am 7 years old.

I am safest when I play in my imagination. I imagine I am a princess, and my daddy's the knight that comes to save me from the dragons.

The dragons are the ones who hurt me. They make fun of me.

The dragons make fun of lots of things, but mostly my scars. I got my scars from falling down the stairs outside our house when I was 2 years old. They are smaller than they used to be, but they haven't changed in a long time.

I remember my mommy kissing my scars and telling me how beautiful and strong I am. But Mommy can't do that anymore because Mommy got sick and passed when I was 3.

Whenever I am sad, my daddy holds me in his arms and tells me I am special.

Every Sunday we go to church. I love to watch the children's choir sing songs of praise.

I wish I could stand up there with them, singing, but I am too scared.

I am too scared of what everyone will see when they look at me.

I get scared thinking about the dragons making fun of me because I might make a mistake and sing the wrong notes. Or because all they can see are my scars. But they don't know I have other scars on the inside – ones you can't see.

When I think about the dragons, my hands start shaking and sweating. My heart beats so hard in my chest, it feels like it's dancing behind my teeth and on top of my tongue.

I get mad and I get sad because I don't understand. Why is this happening? I start looking around and I can't even find my daddy, my knight, my protector, who can make everything okay.

It feels like the walls of the church are all falling on me. I cannot move. Worst of all, in my head I can hear the dragons laughing at me.

I start clenching and grinding my teeth. Then suddenly I hear, "Kenya, baby girl, is everything alright?"

I look to the side where I hear his voice. He's my daddy, my knight! I jump into his arms and do not let go until the church services are over.

When I was riding in the car with Daddy, I asked him why the other children laughed at me and made jokes about Mommy passing. "Was it my fault?" I wondered.

I asked him if he thought I was ugly because, when I look in the mirror, I only see scars on my face. I told him how I felt when I had to be around other people. I began to cry. When I ask him things like this, he always smiles at me and says, "No matter what, you are strong." But I sure don't feel strong.

At school, I started writing stories about a beautiful and brave girl I named Nzinga. She was the kind of girl I wished I could be. Like me, she could sing. And sometimes the dragons made fun of Nzinga too. But Nzinga confronted her dragons. She talked back to the mean mirrors, telling them that the scars on her face show how strong she is. It's like she had warrior powers. Nzinga had no weaknesses. Her hands did not shake. Her heart had a nice, calm beat.

On Saturday, Daddy invited a friend to our house. She told me her name was Dr. Phillips and that she works with unique children like me. Dad told me to tell her about my thoughts and feelings. Daddy also told her I was writing about a warrior named Nzinga. She asked me if it was okay for her to read my short stories. After she read my stories, she told Daddy and me that I had something called anxiety. She said anxiety is something that a lot of people deal with, and I had been through a lot. Maybe the anxiety is because my mom went away. Or maybe it's just part of who I am. But she said that no matter what, I am "special, strong, and did nothing wrong."

That night, Daddy told me he thought I was just like Nzinga and nothing in the world could stop me from singing or from confronting my dragons, or what he called bullies.

I visited with Dr. Phillips a lot at first. Then a little bit less over time. She gave me things to practice and think about.

One night I dreamed of Nzinga and my mommy. They came together and told me it was time for me to do it – to sing – and to confront those dragons. Just like Dr. Phillips, they told me I was special, strong, and did nothing wrong. They told me to always remember those words whenever I felt my heart pound and when my hands would sweat and shake.

The next morning, I walked into church. One of my dragons began to make fun of the scars on my face. I told her I was special and strong. I told her I did nothing wrong. I walked away smiling. I told the minister I wanted to sing. I told him it was a gift that my mommy said I had. I could not believe he said yes and that he would love to hear my voice.

When church began, the minister told everyone that I had a gift to share with them. He told me to come forward. Daddy looked at me, shocked and surprised. The walls that I worried would cave in began to fade, and I began to repeat what Mommy and Nzinga told me.

Before I knew it, I was singing. The song was one of Momma's favorite church songs. I am no longer afraid of what people think when they look at me. No longer do I hide my gift of song because I am afraid of hitting a wrong note. After the song, I told everyone that my mommy, daddy, and Nzinga had said that I was special, strong, and did nothing wrong.

I smiled when I said it. I finally believed it! Walking back to my seat, I said to myself, "Kenya, you are special, strong, and you did nothing wrong. ***Fly, butterfly, fly!***"

My name is Abbas Kidjo.

I was born in Kenya, a country in Africa. I am 9 years old. My family recently moved to the United States. It is very different here.

I am an only child. I often feel lonely. It is not easy for me to make friends. I feel like I am different from other kids.

When I am thinking, lots of ideas go through my brain. I get so excited about what I am thinking. I want to get everything out. Sometimes the other kids say, "You talk too fast," or they frown at me as if I am making them angry. It makes me ashamed, like I am doing something wrong.

On my first day of school, I met my teacher. Then I saw the kids in my class. Some of them looked very different than the kids I went to school with in Africa. Some of them sounded different and spoke different languages.

In class, we have reading time. Different kids have to go up to the front of the class and read from a book chosen by the teacher. But I have a problem.

When the other kids start to read, I start thinking about other stuff like being back in Africa playing games with my friends. Then I hear the teacher call my name, "Abbas. It's your turn to read. Pick up where we left off."

Oh, that is right. I am in school, and it is my turn to read. But I do not know what I am supposed to read. When the teacher asks, "Abbas, were you paying attention?" I have to say no. But I really am trying. I cannot stop my brain from thinking about other stuff. I can tell the teacher is starting to get mad at me. It keeps happening over and over. And the kids start to hurt my feelings. I hear them say, "Can we skip him?" or "Not again!" I cannot help it. It is not my fault.

Whenever I try to read a book, the words just fly off the pages.

It is so hard for me to concentrate like the other kids in class.

When we do our schoolwork, I start daydreaming. Sometimes I get out of my seat and wander around.

"Abbas, right now you should be in your seat. Please sit down, Abbas," my teacher reminds me. So I go back to my desk, but it is so hard for me to stay still.

I try, try, and try some more but I cannot help it.

I do think I am a bad boy. I know I am sitting here in the classroom, but my mind is somewhere else.

Today I came to school and, to my surprise, saw Mommy and Daddy there. I ran up to them and gave them a big hug. "What are you doing here?" I asked.

"The teacher called us to a meeting to talk," Dad said.

"Did I do something wrong?" I wondered.

"No, son, we just want to talk to the teachers and staff to make sure you can do your best at school," Mom said.

In the meeting, my teacher talked about those times when she would ask me to read aloud and I had a hard time finding my place.

There was a man named Dr. Strong who said he was a "school psychologist." He told me and my parents that I had something called ADHD.

"What is that?" I asked.

"ADHD makes your mind go on little trips. It is a little like when Mommy and Daddy put you in the car and you go places. Only it is your thoughts that are going places," Dr. Strong said. "While you are traveling, you sometimes miss the reading that is going on in class. The good news is that there are ways we can help you not miss what is being taught so you stay focused on the things going on right in front of you."

Dr. Strong gave me a book filled with blank writing paper and told me that I was going to use this as my Little Thought Book.

"Every time your thought goes away to somewhere else, use this book to write down what you are thinking about. Writing it down helps your brain know that it will not forget anything important and that you can get back to it later. Then count to five. When you get to five, try to focus your mind back on your schoolwork and what is going on in class. It's okay if you have trouble refocusing. The more you practice, the better you will get," Dr. Strong said.

My therapist encouraged me too: "You are not a bad boy. You are special, strong, and you did nothing wrong. It might take some time to figure it all out, but we'll work together and make sure you get the help you need."

"I am not a bad boy," I repeated, with a smile on my face. "I am special, strong, and I did nothing wrong! *Fly, butterfly, fly!*"

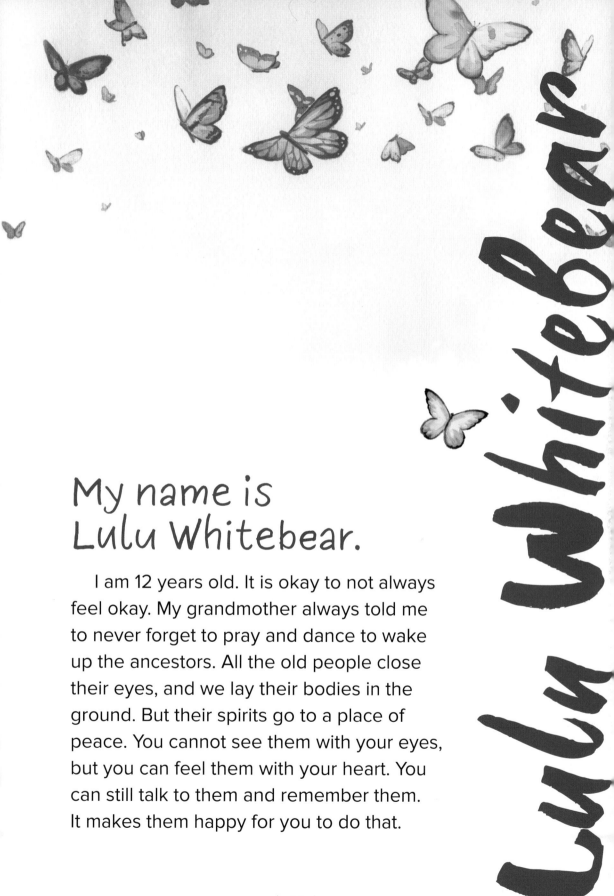

My name is Lulu Whitebear.

I am 12 years old. It is okay to not always feel okay. My grandmother always told me to never forget to pray and dance to wake up the ancestors. All the old people close their eyes, and we lay their bodies in the ground. But their spirits go to a place of peace. You cannot see them with your eyes, but you can feel them with your heart. You can still talk to them and remember them. It makes them happy for you to do that.

My grandmother was my best friend. We did everything together.

She made my clothes with her own hands and told me how each part of the fabric and the colors said something beautiful about me, our family, and our people. She told me to never be embarrassed about who I was created to be. Because of her, I embrace and love my culture.

We would play hide-and-seek, and she would let me win. I enjoyed being around her.

She would read me stories about courageous people.

"Lulu, I am reading these stories to you so you will be knowledgeable and proud of the strength of the women that came before you. Always remember, you are capable of anything your heart desires."

Grandmother also told me that no matter what, she would always be with me.

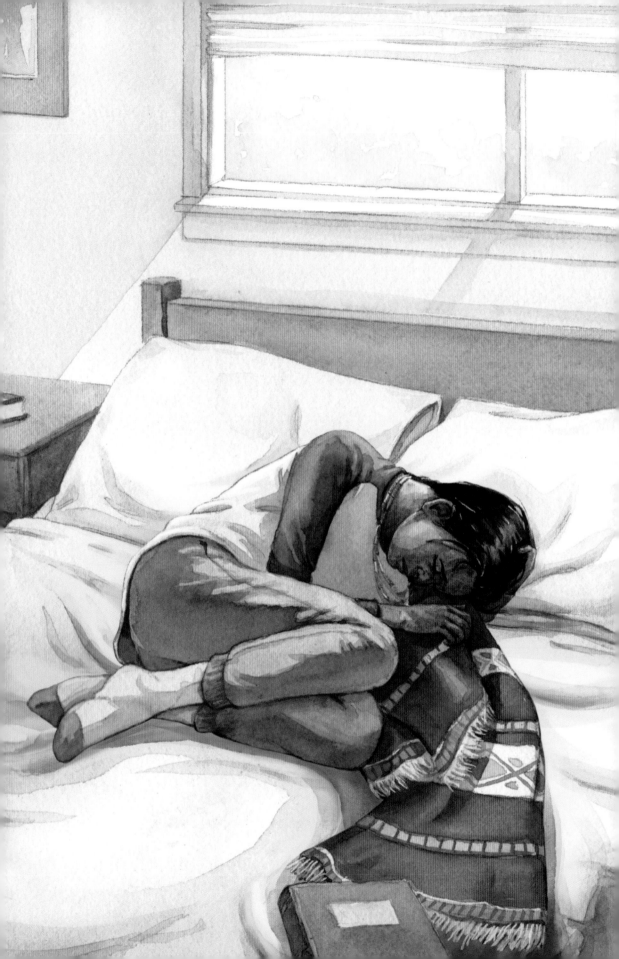

One day, she became sick. She was coughing. She started losing weight. She lost all her beautiful hair.

She did not have enough energy to speak, so she would just hold my hand and kiss me. I would rest my head on her chest. I could tell it was hard for her to breathe.

It was on a warm Sunday when Mom told me my grandmother had gone to the peaceful place but to remember that she loved me. I cried all day. Then I started crying every day. I did not feel strong. I missed my best friend. I knew she was at peace, but it hurt because I could not be with her.

I could not get out of bed because my body was sore. I could not eat, and all I did was sleep. I did not want to go out and play hide-and-seek because I knew she would not be there.

My parents worried about me and said they were going to try to help.

They dressed me up and took me to meet a man who said he was a therapist and worked in our community. He asked me questions, and then he said I had something called depression. He told me that depression was feeling bad, but not just for a little while. He said when people are depressed, it's hard for them to do the things they usually do. He said things happen to us in life that can make us feel that way, like when people we love go to the peaceful place. We miss them and that is okay. But sometimes we miss them so much that we lose all our energy and hurt like someone is squeezing our hearts too tight. Sometimes it gets better by itself, but other times we need help to feel better. The therapist told me he and my parents would work together to help me.

The therapist also said I could help myself get better. Instead of getting in bed every time I thought about my grandmother, I should think of something she would want me to do. Grandmother always told me to honor my culture, so I should try to do things that honor our culture and honor her. I could get my notebook and write about the stories she told me and then share them with other kids. I will not go to bed until I feel sleepy. I learned that I could turn sad time into happy, productive time.

My parents hugged me and told me it was okay to not always feel okay. They said they loved me and were there to help and that I did nothing wrong. Mom said she missed Grandma, too.

I closed my eyes. It was like my grandmother was right next to me. I heard her voice telling me, "Lulu, you are special, strong, and you did nothing wrong."

As we left the therapist's office, I kept repeating to myself that I was special, strong, and did nothing wrong until I believed it.

On the way home, I looked up at the sky and said, "Thank you, Grandmother, for always reminding me of the strength of the women before me. I am special like you, strong like them, and I did nothing wrong for you to go away. I miss you, and I love you. ***Fly, butterfly, fly!***"

Boys Town Press books

Resources for counselors, educators, and families

Each main character in this anthology is managing a common yet challenging mental health diagnosis. To learn more about these diagnoses and for tools and resources for children, caregivers, and professionals, be sure to use the accompanying supplemental guides.

978-1-944882-84-6

978-1-944882-85-3

A book series and accompanying activity guides focused on childhood friendships, finding your place, advocating for yourself, and being true to who you are.

Jennifer Licate
GRADES 4-8

978-1-944882-63-1

978-1-944882-65-5

978-1-944882-67-9

BoysTownPress.org

For information on Boys Town, its Education Model®, Common Sense Parenting®, and training programs:
boystowntraining.org, boystown.org/parenting
training@BoysTown.org, 1-800-545-5771

For parenting and educational books and other resources:
BoysTownPress.org, btpress@BoysTown.org, 1-800-282-6657